# DOORWAY TO
# KAL-JMAR

# DOORWAY TO KAL-JMAR

by Damon Knight

*Two men had died before Syme Rector's guns to give him the key to the ancient city of Kal-Jmar—a city of untold wealth, and of robots that made desires instant commands.*

The tall man loitered a moment before a garish window display, his eyes impassive in his space-burned face, as the Lillis patrolman passed. Then he turned, burying his long chin in the folds of his sand cape, and took up the pursuit of the dark figure ahead once more.

Above, the city's multicolored lights were reflected from the translucent Dome—a distant, subtly distorted Lillis, through which the stars shone dimly.

Getting through that dome had been his first urgent problem, but now he had another, and a more pressing one. It had been simple enough to pass himself off as an itinerant prospector and gain entrance to the city, after his ship had crashed in the Mare Cimmerium. But the rest would not be so simple. He had to acquire a spaceman's identity card, and he had to do it fast. It was only a matter of time until the Triplanet Patrol gave up the misleading trail he had made into the hill country, and concluded that he must have reached Lillis. After that, his only safety lay in shipping out on a freighter as soon as possible. He had to get off Mars, because his trail was warm, and the Patrol thorough.

They knew, of course, that he was an outlaw—the very fact of the crashed, illegally-armed ship would have told them that. But they didn't know that he was Syme Rector, the most-wanted and most-feared raider in the System. In that was his only advantage.

He walked a little faster, as his quarry turned up a side street and then boarded a moving ramp to an upper level. He watched until the short, wide-shouldered figure in spaceman's harness disappeared over the top of the ramp, and then followed.

The man was waiting for him at the mouth of the ascending tunnel.

Syme looked at him casually, without a flicker of expression, and started to walk on, but the other stepped into his path. He was quite young, Syme saw, with a fighter's shoulders under the white leather, and a hard, determined thrust to his firm jaw.

"All right," the boy said quietly. "What is it?"

"I don't understand," Syme said.

"The game, the angle. You've been following me. Do you want trouble?"

"Why, no," Syme told him bewilderedly. "I haven't been following you. I—"

# DOORWAY TO KAL-JMAR

The boy knuckled his chin reflectively. "You could be lying," he said finally. "But maybe I've made a mistake." Then—"Okay, citizen, you can clear—but don't let me catch you on my tail again."

Syme murmured something and turned away, feeling the spaceman's eyes on the small of his back until he turned the corner. At the next street he took a ramp up, crossed over and came down on the other side a block away. He waited until he saw the boy's broad figure pass the intersection, and then followed again more cautiously.

It was risky, but there was no other way. The signatures, the data, even the photograph on the card could be forged once Syme got his hands on it, but the identity card itself—that oblong of dark diamondite, glowing with the tiny fires of radioactivity—that could not be imitated, and the only way to get it was to kill.

Up ahead was the Founders' Tower, the tallest building in Lillis. The boy strode into the entrance lobby, bought a ticket for the observation platform, and took the elevator. As soon as his car was out of sight in the transparent tube, Syme followed. He put a half-credit slug into the machine, took the punctured slip of plastic that came out. The ticket went into a scanning slot in the wall of the car, and the elevator whisked him up.

*

The tower was high, more than a hundred meters above the highest level of the city, and the curved dome that kept air in Lillis was close overhead. Syme looked up, after his first appraising glance about the platform, and saw the bright-blue pinpoint of Earth. The sight stirred a touch of nostalgia in him, as it always did, but he put it aside.

The boy was hunched over the circular balustrade a little distance away. Except for him, the platform was empty. Syme loosened his slim, deadly energy pistol in its holster and padded catlike toward the silent figure.

It was over in a minute. The boy whirled as he came up, warned by some slight sound, or by the breath of Syme's passage in the still air. He opened his mouth to shout, and brought up his arm in a swift, instinctive gesture. But the blow never landed. Syme's pistol spat its silent white pencil of flame, and the boy crumpled to the floor with a minute, charred hole in the white leather over his chest.

Syme stooped over him swiftly, found a thick wallet and thrust it into his pocket without a second glance. Then he raised the body in his arms and thrust it over the parapet.

It fell, and in the same instant Syme felt a violent tug at his wrist. Before he could move to stop himself, he was over the edge. Too late, he realized what had happened—one of the hooks on the dead spaceman's harness had caught the heavy wristband of his chronometer. He was falling, linked to the body of his victim!

Hardly knowing what he did, he lashed out wildly with his other arm, felt his fingertips catch and bite into the edge of the balustrade. His body hit the wall of the tower with a thump, and, a second later, the corpse below him hit the wall. Then they both hung there, swaying a little and Syme's fingers slipped a little with each motion.

Gritting his teeth, he brought the magnificent muscles of his arm into play, raising the forearm against the dead weight of the dangling body. Fraction by slow fraction of an inch, it came up. Syme could feel the sweat pouring from his brow, running saltily into his eyes. His arms felt as if they were being torn from their sockets. Then the hook slipped free, and the tearing, unbearable weight vanished.

The reaction swung Syme against the building again, and he almost lost his slippery hold on the balustrade. After a moment he heard the spaceman's body strike with a squashy thud, somewhere below.

He swung up his other arm, got a better grip on the balustrade. He tried cautiously to get a leg up, but the motion loosened his hold on the smooth surface again. He relaxed, thinking furiously. He could hold on for another minute at most; then it was the final blast-off.

He heard running footsteps, and then a pale face peered over the ledge at him. He realized suddenly that the whole incident could have taken only a few seconds. He croaked, "Get me up."

Wordlessly, the man clasped thin fingers around his wrist. The other pulled, with much puffing and panting, and with his help Syme managed to get a leg over the edge and hoist his trembling body to safety.

"Are you all right?"

Syme looked at the man, nursing the tortured muscles of his arms. His rescuer was tall and thin, of indeterminate age. He had light, sandy hair, a sharp nose, and—oddly conflicting—pale, serious eyes and a humorous wide mouth. He was still panting.

"I'm not hurt," Syme said. He grinned, his white teeth flashing in his dark, lean face. "Thanks for giving me a hand."

"You scared hell out of me," said the man. "I heard a thud. I thought—you'd gone over." He looked at Syme questioningly.

"That was my bag," the outlaw said quickly. "It slipped out of my hand, and I overbalanced myself when I grabbed for it."

The man sighed. "I need a drink. *You* need a drink. Come on." He picked up a small black suitcase from the floor and started for the elevator, then stopped. "Oh—your bag. Shouldn't we do something about that?"

"Never mind," said Syme, taking his arm. "The shock must have busted it wide open. My laundry is probably all over Lillis by now."

They got off at the amusement level, three tiers down, and found a cafe around the corner. Syme wasn't worried about the man he had just killed. He had heard no second thud, so the body must have stayed on the first outcropping of the tower it struck. It probably wouldn't be found until morning.

And he had the wallet. When he paid for the first round of *culcha*, he took it out and stole a glance at the identification card inside. There it was—his ticket to freedom. He began feeling expansive, and even friendly toward the slender, mouse-like man across the table. It was the *culcha*, of course. He knew it, and didn't care. In the morning he'd find a freighter berth—in as big a spaceport as Lillis, there were always jobs open. Meanwhile, he might as well enjoy himself, and it was safer to be seen with a companion than to be alone.

He listened lazily to what the other was saying, leaning his tall, graceful body back into the softly-cushioned seat.

"Lissen," said Harold Tate. He leaned forward on one elbow, slipped, caught himself, and looked at the elbow reproachfully. "Lissen," he said again, "I trust you, Jones. You're obvi-obviously an adventurer, but you have an honest face. I can't see it very well at the moment, but I hic!—pardon—seem to recall it as an honest face. I'm going to tell you something, because I need your help!—help." He paused. "I need a guide. D'you know this part of Mars well?"

"Sure," said Syme absently. Out in the center of the floor, an AG plate had been turned on. Five Venusian girls were diving and twisting in its influence, propelling themselves by the motion of their delicately-webbed feet and trailing long gauzy streamers of synthesilk after them. Syme watched them through narrowed lids, feeling the glow of *culcha* inside him.

"I wanta go to Kal-Jmar," said Tate.

Syme snapped to attention, every nerve tingling. An indefinable sense, a hunch that had served him well before, told him that something big was coming—something that promised adventure and loot for Syme Rector. "Why?" he asked softly. "Why to Kal-Jmar?"

Harold Tate told him, and later, when Syme had taken him to his rooms, he showed him what was in his little black suitcase. Syme had been right; it was big.

*

Kal-Jmar was the riddle of the Solar System. It was the only remaining city of the ancient Martian race—the race that, legends said, had risen to greater heights than any other Solar culture. The machines, the artifacts, the records of the Martians were all there, perfectly preserved inside the city's bubble-like dome, after God knew how many thousands of years. But they couldn't be reached.

For Kal-Jmar's dome was not the thing of steelite that protected Lillis: it was a tenuous, globular field of force that defied analysis as it defied explosives and diamond drills. The field extended both above and below the ground, and tunneling was of no avail. No one knew what had happened to the Martians, whether they were the ancestors of the present decadent Martian race, or a different species. No one knew anything about them or about Kal-Jmar.

In the early days, when the conquest of Mars was just beginning, Earth scientists had been wild to get into the city. They had observed it from every angle, taken photographs of its architecture and the robots that still patrolled its fantastically winding streets, and then they had tried everything they knew to pierce the wall.

Later, however, when every unsuccessful attempt had precipitated a bloody uprising of the present-day Martians—resulting in a rapid dwindling of the number of Martians—the Mars Protectorate had stepped in and forbidden any further experiments; forbidden, in fact, any Earthman to go near the place.

Thus matter had stood for over a hundred years, until Harold Tate. Tate, a physicist, had stumbled on a field that seemed to be identical in properties to the Kal-Jmar dome; and what is more, he had found a force that would break it down.

And so he had made his first trip to Mars, and within twenty-four hours, by the blindest of chances, blurted out his secret to Syme Rector, the scourge of the spaceways, the man with a thousand credits on his sleek, tigerish head.

Syme's smile was not tigerish now; it was carefully, studiedly mild. For Tate was no longer drunk, and it was important that it should not occur to him that he had been indiscreet.

"This is native territory we're coming to, Harold," he said. "Better strap on your gun."

"Why. Are they really dangerous?"

"They're unpredictable," Syme told him. "They're built differently, and they think differently. They breathe like us, down in their caverns where there's air, but they also eat sand, and get their oxygen that way."

"Yes, I've heard about that," Tate said. "Iron oxide—very interesting metabolism." He got his energy pistol out of the compartment and strapped it on absently.

Syme turned the little sand car up a gentle rise towards the tortuous hill country in the distance. "Not only that," he continued. "They eat the damndest stuff. Lichens and fungi and tumble-grass off the deserts—all full of deadly poisons, from arsenic up the line to xopite. They seem intelligent enough—in their own way—but they never come near our cities and they either can't or won't learn Terrestrial. When the first colonists came here, they had to learn *their* crazy language. Every word of it can mean any one of a dozen different things, depending on the inflection you give it. I can speak it some, but not much. Nobody can. We don't think the same."

"So you think they might attack us?" Tate asked again, nervously.

"They *might* do anything," Syme said curtly. "Don't worry about it."

The hills were much closer than they had seemed, because of Mars' deceptively low horizon. In half an hour they were in the midst of a wilderness of fantastically eroded dunes and channels, laboring on sliding treads up the sides of steep hills only to slither down again on the other side.

\*

Syme stopped the car abruptly as a deep, winding channel appeared across their path. "Gully," he announced. "Shall we cross it, or follow it?"

Tate peered through the steelite nose of the car. "Follow, I guess," he offered. "It seems to go more or less where we're going, and if we cross it we'll only come to a couple dozen more."

Syme nodded and moved the sand car up to the edge of the gully. Then he pressed a stud on the control board; a metal arm extruded from the tail of the car and a heavy spike slowly unscrewed from it, driving deep into the sand. A light on the board flashed, indicating that the spike was in and would bear the car's weight, and Syme started the car over the edge.

10

As the little car nosed down into the gully, the metal arm left behind revealed itself to be attached to a length of thick, very strong wire cable, with a control cord inside. They inched down the almost vertical incline, unreeling the cable behind them, and starting minor landslides as they descended.

Finally they touched bottom. Syme pressed another stud, and above, the metal spike that had supported them screwed itself out of the ground again and the cable reeled in.

Tate had been watching with interest. "Very ingenious," he said. "But how do we get up again?"

"Most of these gullies peter out gradually," said Syme, "but if we want or have to climb out where it's deep, we have a little harpoon gun that shoots the anchor up on top."

"Good. I shouldn't like to stay down here for the rest of my natural life. Depressing view." He looked up at the narrow strip of almost-black sky visible from the floor of the gully, and shook his head.

Neither Syme nor Tate ever had a chance to test the efficiency of their harpoon gun. They had traveled no more than five hundred meters, and the gully was as deep as ever, when Tate, looking up, saw a deeper blackness blot out part of the black sky directly overhead. He shouted, "Look out!" and grabbed for the nearest steering lever.

The car wheeled around in a half circle and ran into the wall of the gully. Syme was saying, "What—?" when there was a thunderous crash that shook the sturdy walls of the car, as a huge boulder smashed into the ground immediately to their left.

When the smoky red dust had cleared away, they saw that the left tread of the sand car was crushed beyond all recognition.

Syme was cursing slowly and steadily with a deep, seething anger. Tate said, "I guess we walk from here on." Then he looked up again and caught a glimpse of the horde of beasts that were rushing up the gully toward them.

"My God!" he said. "What are those?"

Syme looked. "Those," he said bitterly, "are Martians."

The natives, like all Martian fauna, were multi-legged. Also like all Martian fauna, they moved so fast that you couldn't see how many legs they did have. Actually, however, the natives had six legs apiece—or, more properly, four legs and two arms. Their lungs were not as large as they appeared, being collapsed at the moment.

What caused the bulge that made their torsos look like sausages was a huge air bladder, with a valve arrangement from the stomach and feeding directly into the bloodstream.

Their faces were vaguely canine, but the foreheads were high, and the lips were not split. They did resemble dogs, in that their thick black fur was splotched with irregulate patches of white. These patches of white were subject to muscular control and could be spread out fanwise; or, conversely, the black could be expanded to cover the white, which helped to take care of the extremes of Martian temperature. Right now they were mostly black.

The natives slowed down and spread out to surround the wrecked sand car, and it could be seen that most of them were armed with spears, although some had the slim Benson energy guns—strictly forbidden to Martians.

Syme stopped cursing and watched tensely. Tate said nothing, but he swallowed audibly.

One Martian, who looked exactly like all the rest, stepped forward and motioned unmistakably for the two to come out. He waited a moment and then gestured with his energy gun. That gun, Syme knew from experience, could burn through a small thickness of steelite if held on the same spot long enough.

*

"Come on," Syme said grimly. He rose and reached for a pressure suit, and Tate followed him.

"What do you think they'll—" he began, and then stopped himself. "I know. They're unpredictable."

"Yeah," said Syme, and opened the door. The air in the car *whooshed* into the near-vacuum outside, and he and Tate stepped out.

The Martian leader looked at them enigmatically, then turned and started off. The other natives closed in on them, and they all bounded along under the weak gravity.

They bounded along for what Syme figured as a good kilometer and a half, and they then reached a branch in the gully and turned down it, going lower all the time. Under the light of their helmet lamps, they could see the walls of the gully—a tunnel, now—getting darker and more solid. Finally, when Syme estimated they were about nine kilometers down, there was even a suggestion of moisture.

The tunnel debouched at last into a large cavern. There was a phosphorescent gleam from fungus along the walls, but Syme couldn't decide how far away the far wall was. He noticed something else, though.

"There's air here," he said to Tate. "I can see dust motes in it." He switched his helmet microphone from radio over to the audio membrane on the outside of the helmet. "*Kalis methra*," he began haltingly, "*seltin guna getal.*"

"Yes, there is air here," said the Martian leader, startlingly. "Not enough for your use, however, so do not open your helmets."

Syme swore amazedly.

"I thought you said they didn't speak Terrestrial," Tate said. Syme ignored him.

"We had our reasons for not doing so," the Martian said.

"But how—?"

"We are telepaths, of course. On a planet which is nearly airless on its surface, we have to be. A tendency of the Terrestrial mind is to ignore the obvious. We have not had a spoken language of our own for several thousand years."

He darted a glance at Syme's darkly scowling face. His own hairy face was expressionless, but Syme sensed that he was amused. "Yes, you're right," he said. "The language you and your fellows struggled to learn is a fraud, a hodge-podge concocted to deceive you."

Tate looked interested. "But why this—this gigantic masquerade?"

"You had nothing to give us," the Martian said simply.

Tate frowned, then flushed. "You mean you avoided revealing yourselves because you—had nothing to gain from mental intercourse with us?"

"Yes."

Tate thought again. "But—"

"No," the Martian interrupted him, "revealing the extent of our civilization would have spared us nothing at your people's hands. Yours is an imperialist culture, and you would have had Mars, whether you thought you were taking it from equals or not."

"Never mind that," Syme broke in impatiently. "What do you want with us?"

The Martian looked at him appraisingly. "You already suspect. Unfortunately, you must die."

\*

It was a weird situation, Syme thought. His mind was racing, but as yet he could see no way out. He began to wonder, if he did, could he keep the Martians from

13

knowing about it? Then he realized that the Martian must have received that thought, too, and he was enraged. He stood, holding himself in check with an effort.

"Will you tell us why?" Tate asked.

"You were brought here for that purpose. It is part of our conception of justice. I will tell you and your—friend—anything you wish to know."

Syme noticed that the other Martians had retired to the farther side of the cavern. Some were munching the glowing fungus. That left only the leader, who was standing alertly on all fours a short distance away from them, holding the Benson gun trained on them. Syme tried not to think about the gun, especially about making a grab for it. It was like trying not to think of the word "hippopotamus."

Tate squatted down comfortably on the floor of the cavern, apparently unconcerned, but his hands were trembling slightly. "First why—" he began.

"There are many secrets in Kal-Jmar," the Martian said, "among them a very simple catalyzing agent which could within fifty years transform Mars to a planet with Terrestrially-thick atmosphere."

"I think I see," Tate said thoughtfully. "That's been the ultimate aim all along, but so far the problem has us licked. If we solved it, then we'd have all of Mars, not just the cities. Your people would die out. You couldn't have that, of course."

He sighed deeply. He spread his gloved hands before him and looked at them with a queer intentness. "Well—how about the Martians—the Kal-Jmar Martians, I mean? I'd dearly love to know the answer to that one."

"Neither of the alternatives in your mind is correct. They were not a separate species, although they were unlike us. But they were not our ancestors, either. They were the contemporaries of our ancestors."

"Several thousand years ago Mars' loss of atmosphere began to make itself felt. There were two ways out. Some chose to seal themselves into cities like Kal-Jmar; our ancestors chose to adapt their bodies to the new conditions. Thus the race split. Their answer to the problem was an evasion; they remained static. Our answer was the true one, for we progressed. We progressed beyond the need of science; they remained its slaves. They died of a plague—and other causes.

"You see," he finished gently, "our deception has caused a natural confusion in your minds. They were the degenerates, not we."

"And yet," Tate mused, "you are being destroyed by contact with an—inferior—culture."

"We hope to win yet," the Martian said.

Tate stood up, his face very white. "Tell me one thing," he begged. "Will our two races ever live together in amity?"

The Martian lowered his head. "That is for unborn generations." He looked at Tate again and aimed the energy gun. "You are a brave man," he said. "I am sorry."

Syme saw all his hopes of treasure and glory go glimmering down the sights of the Martian's Benson gun, and suddenly the pent-up rage in him exploded. Too swiftly for his intention to be telegraphed, before he knew himself what he meant to do, he hurled himself bodily into the Martian.

*

It was like tangling with a draft horse. The Martian was astonishingly strong. Syme scrambled desperately for the gun, got it, but couldn't tear it out of the Martian's fingers. And all the time he could almost feel the Martian's telepathic call for help surging out. He heard the swift pad of his followers coming across the cavern.

He put everything he had into one mighty, murderous effort. Every muscle fiber in his superbly trained body crackled and surged with power. He roared his fury. And the gun twisted out of the Martian's iron grip!

He clubbed the prostrate leader with it instantly, then reversed the weapon and snapped a shot at the nearest Martian. The creature dropped his lance and fell without a sound.

The next instant a ray blinked at him, and he rolled out of the way barely in time. The searing ray cut a swath over the leader's body and swerved to cut down on him. Still rolling, he fired at the holder of the weapon. The gun dropped and winked out on the floor.

Syme jumped to his feet and faced his enemies, snarling like the trapped tiger he was. Another ray slashed at him, and he bent lithely to let it whistle over his head. Another, lower this time. He flipped his body into the air and landed upright, his gun still blazing. His right leg burned fiercely from a ray-graze, but he ignored it. And all the while he was mowing down the massed natives in great swaths, seeking out the ones armed with Bensons in swift, terrible slashes, dodging spears and other missiles in midair, and roaring at the top of his powerful lungs.

At last there were none with guns left to oppose him. He scythed down the rest in two terrible, lightning sweeps of his ray, then dropped the weapon from blistered fingers.

He was gasping for breath, and realized that he was losing air from the seared-open right leg of his suit. He reached for the emergency kit at his side, drawing in great, gasping breaths, and fumbled out a tube of sealing liquid. He spread the stuff on liberally, smearing it impartially over flesh and fabric. It felt like liquid hell on the burned, bleeding leg, but he kept on until the quick-drying fluid formed an airtight patch.

Only then did he turn, to see Tate flattened against the wall behind him, his hands empty at his sides. "I'm sorry," Tate said miserably. "I could have grabbed a spear or something, but—I just couldn't, not even to save my own life. I—I halfway hoped they'd kill both of us."

Syme glared at him and spat, too enraged to think of diplomacy. He turned and strode out of the cavern, carrying his right leg stiffly, but with his feral, tigerish head held high.

He led the way, wordlessly, back to the wrecked sand car. Tate followed him with a hangdog, beaten air, as though he had just found something that shattered all his previous concepts of the verities in life, and didn't know what to do about it.

Still silently, Syme refilled his oxygen tank, watched Tate do the same, and then picked up two spare tanks and the precious black suitcase and handed one of the tanks to Tate. Then he stumped around to the back of the car and inspected the damage. The cable reel, which might have drawn them out of the gully, was hopelessly smashed. That was that.

*

They started off down the canyon, Syme urging the slighter man to a fast clip, even though his leg was already stiffening. When they finally reached a climbable spot, Syme was limping badly and Tate was obviously exhausted.

They clambered wearily out onto the level sands again just as the small, blazing sun was setting. "Luck," grunted Syme. "Our only chance of getting near the city is at night." He peered around, shading his eyes from the sun's glare with a gauntleted hand. "See that?"

Following his pointing finger, Tate saw a faint, ephemeral arc showing above a line of low hills in the distance. "Kal-Jmar," said Syme.

Tate brightened a little. His body was too filled with fatigue for his mind to do any work on the problem that was baffling him, and so it receded into the back of his mind.

"Kal-Jmar," whispered Syme again.

16

There was no twilight. The sun dropped abruptly behind the low horizon, and darkness fell, sudden and absolute. Syme picked up the extra oxygen tank and the suitcase, checked his direction by a wrist compass, and started toward the hills. Tate rose wearily to his feet and followed again.

Two hours later, Kal-Jmar stood before them. They had wormed their way past the sentry posts, doing most of the last two hundred meters on all fours. With skill and luck, and with Syme's fierce, burning determination, they had managed to escape detection—and there they were. Journey's end.

Tate stared up at the shining, starlight towers in speechless admiration. If the people who had built this city had been decadent, still their architecture was magnificent. The city was a rhapsody made solid. There was a sense of decay about it, he thought, but it was the decay of supreme beauty, caught at the very verge of dissolution and preserved for all eternity.

"Well?" demanded Syme.

Tate started, shaken out of his dream. He looked down at the black suitcase, a little wonderingly, and then pulled it to him and opened it.

Inside, carefully wrapped in shock-absorbing tissue, was a fragile contrivance of many tubes and wires, and a tiny parabolic mirror. It had a brand new Elecorp 210 volt battery, and it needed every volt of that tremendous power. Tate made the connections, his hands trembling slightly, and set it up on a telescoping tripod. Syme watched him closely, his big body tensed with expectation.

The field was before them, shimmering faintly in the starlight. It looked unsubstantial as the stuff of dreams, but both men knew that no power man possessed, unless it was the thing Tate held, could penetrate that screen.

Tate set the mechanism up close to the field, aimed it very delicately, and closed a minute switch. After a long second, he opened it again.

Nothing happened.

The screen was still there, as unsubstantial and as solid as ever. There was no change.

*

Tate looked worriedly at his wiring, a deep wrinkle appearing between his pale, serious eyes. Syme stood stock-still but quivering with repressed energy, scowling like a thundercloud.

"It must be capable of working," Tate told himself querulously. "The Martians knew—they wouldn't have tried to stop us if—Wait a minute." He paced back and forth, biting his lip. Syme watched him with catlike eyes, clenching and unclenching his great fists.

Tate paused. "I think I have it," he said slowly. "I haven't enough power to hetrodyne the whole screen, although that's theoretically possible. But there must be weaker portions of the field—doors—set to open on the impact of a beam like this one. But I've only got power enough for two more tries. Jones, where would you put an entrance, if you'd built Kal-Jmar?"

Syme's eyes widened, and he stared around slowly. "A thousand years ago?" he muttered. "Two thousand? These hills were raised in five hundred. We can't go by topography.

"In front of one of the main arteries, then. But there are dozens, no one larger than the other. Did they have dozens of doors?"

"Maybe," said Tate. He pointed to the right, where the fairy towers of Kal-Jmar swept aside to leave a broad avenue. "It's the nearest—as good as any other."

They walked over to it in silence, and in silence Tate set up his equipment once more. He shifted it from side to side, squinting, until he had it lined up exactly on the center of the avenue. Then he took a long breath, and closed the switch again.

The switch came up. Syme stared with fierce eagerness, eyes ablaze. For a moment there was nothing, and then—

Tate clutched the big man's arm. "Look!" he breathed.

Where the ray from Tate's machine had impinged, a faintly-glowing spot of violet radiance! As they watched it widened, dilating into a perfect circle of violet, enclosing nothingness. The door was opening.

"It worked," Tate said softly. "It worked!"

Syme shook off his grip impatiently, put his hand to the gun in the holster of his suit. Tate was still watching, fascinated. "Look," he said again. "The color is changing slightly, falling down the spectrum. I think that's a warning signal. When it reaches red, the door will close." He moved toward the widening door, like a sleepwalker.

"Wait," Syme said hoarsely. "You forgot the machine."

Tate turned, said, "Oh yes," and walked back. Then he saw the gun in Syme's hand. His jaw dropped slightly, but he didn't say anything. He just stood there, looking dumbly from the gun to Syme's dark face.

Syme shot him carefully in the chest.

He dropped like a rag doll, but Syme's aim had been bad. He wasn't dead yet. He rolled his eyes up, like a child. His lips moved. In spite of himself, Syme bent forward to listen.

"*You'll be—sorry,*" Tate said, and died.

Air was sighing out through the widening hole in the screen. Syme straightened and smiled tolerantly. For a moment, he had been unreasonably afraid of what Tate was about to say. Some detail he had forgotten, perhaps, something that would trap him now that Tate, the man who knew the answers, was dead. But—he'd be sorry!

For what? Another dead fool?

He gathered up the delicate mechanism in one arm, and, filling his deep lungs, stepped forward through the opening.

\*

The towers of dead Kal-Jmar loomed over him in the dusk as he strode like a conqueror down the long-deserted avenue. The city was full of the whisperings of Kal-Jmar's ancient wraiths, but they touched only a corner of his mind. He was filled to overflowing with the bright, glowing joy of conquest. The city was his!

His boots trod an avenue where no foot had fallen these untold eons, yet there was no dust. The city was bright and furbished waiting for him. He was intoxicated. *The city was his!*

There was a gentle ramp leading upward, and Syme followed it, breathing in the manufactured air of his pressure suit like wine. All around him, the city blazed with treasures beyond price.

*It was his!*

The ramp led to a portal set in the side of a shining needle of a building. Syme strode up to the threshold, and the door dilated for him. He stepped inside; the door closed and a soft light glowed on.

There was air here: good, breathable air. A tiny zephyr of it was blowing from some hidden source against his body. Greatly daring, he unfastened the helmet of his suit and flung it back. He breathed in a lungful of it. God, but it was good after that canned stuff! It was a little heady; it made his head swim—but it was good air, excellent air!

He looked around him, measuring, assessing for the first time. This room alone was worth a fortune. There was platinum; in ornaments, set into the walls, in furniture. That would be enough to buy the little things—a new ship, or perhaps even immunity back on Earth. But that was as nothing to the rest of it, the things three worlds would clamor for—the artifacts, the record books, the machines!

He strode about the room, building plan on grandiose plan. He could take back only a little with him at first; but he could return again and again, with Tate's mechanism and new batteries. But he'd explore the city thoroughly before he left. Somewhere there must be weapons. An invincible weapon, perhaps, that a man could carry in his hand. Perhaps even a perfect body screen. With that he wouldn't have to steal away from Mars on a freighter, hiding his loot and his greatness in a dingy engine room. He could walk into a Triplanet ship and order its captain to take him wherever he chose to go!

*

He stood then in the middle of the room, arms akimbo, his head swimming with glory—and remembered suddenly that he was hungry. He felt in the container of his helmet, extracted a couple of food tablets, and popped them into his mouth.

They would take care of his needs, but they didn't satisfy his hunger. No food tablets for him after this! Steaks, wines, souffles.... His mouth began to water at the very thought.

And then the robot rolled on soundless wheels into the room. Syme whirled and saw it only when it was almost upon him. The thing was remarkably lifelike, and for a moment he was startled.

But it was not alive. It was only a Martian feeding-machine, kept in repair all these millennia by other robots. It was not intelligent, and so it did not know that its masters would never return. It did not know, either, that Syme was not a Martian, or that he wanted a steak, and not the distilled liquor of the *xopa* fungus, which still grew in the subterranean gardens of Kal-Jmar. It was capable only of receiving the mental impulse of hunger, and of responding to that impulse.

And so when Syme saw it and opened his mouth in startlement, the robot acted as it had done with its degenerate, slothful masters. Its flexible feeding tube darted out and half down the man's gullet before he could move to avoid it. And down Syme Rector's throat poured a flood of *xopa*-juice, nectar to Martians, but swift, terrible death to human beings....

Outside, the last doorway to Kal-Jmar closed forever, across from the cold body of Tate.